SHARP SHADES

DOING THE
DOUBLE

Look out for other exciting stories
in the *Sharp Shades* series:

A Murder of Crows by Penny Bates
Witness by Anne Cassidy
Blitz by David Orme

DOING THE DOUBLE

Dale and I used to play this game. We called it *Doing the Double*. If a team wins the league and cup, then they do the double. When we did the double, we pretended to be each other. Twins do it to trick people. For a joke.

We hadn't done it for years. But this time it was serious. Really serious...

At that moment I hated football more than ever.

SHARP SHADES

DOING THE DOUBLE

Alan Durant

Evans

Published in 2007 by
Evans Brothers Limited
2A Portman Mansions
Chiltern St
London W1U 6NR

British Library Cataloguing in Publication Data
Durant, Alan, 1958-
   Doing the double. - Abridged ed. - (Sharp
   shades) 1. Twins - Fiction 2. False personation -
   Fiction 3. Young adult fiction
   I. Title
   823.9'14[J]

ISBN 9780237534479

Series Editor: David Belbin
Editor: Julia Moffatt
Designer: Rob Walster
Picture research: Bryony Jones

This abridged edition was first published in its
original form as a *Shades* titles of the same name.

Picture acknowledgments:
istockphoto.com: pp 2, 8, 14, 21, 24, 31, 35, 41, 47
and 52.

Contents

Prologue

Dale and I used to play this game. We called it Doing the Double. If a team wins the league and cup, then they do the double. When we did the double, we pretended to be each other. Twins do it to trick people. For a joke.

We hadn't done it for years. But this time it was serious. Really serious.

I was in the changing room before the semi-final. Strangers kept clapping me on the back.

'Hey, Dale! What's up?' said my team's goalie. No. Not my team. Dale's team: Blackstock Youth.

'I'm not Dale, I'm Joe,' I wanted to say. But I couldn't. I'd promised Dale. I couldn't back out now.

At that moment I hated football more than ever.

Chapter One

I used to love football like Dale still did. It's not surprising. Our dad was Nicky Green. One of the most talented football players of his generation. That's what everyone said. They said it with a sigh, because he hit the booze and flushed all that talent down the toilet. When we were kids, we worshipped our dad. So did every other kid. He could run with the ball. He could pass and shoot with either foot. He had pace and balance and bags of tricks. He made good defenders look clumsy. How could you help but love the guy?

Kids at school would say, 'It must be great to have Nicky Green as your dad.' And in a way it was. When we were small anyway. When he was at the top of his game and

the booze hadn't taken its toll. But
in another way it wasn't that great.
We hardly ever saw him. If he
wasn't training or playing, he was at
some starry event.

Sometimes I longed for a normal
dad. Dad didn't even play football
with us. But Dale and I were
naturals. We learnt a lot from
playing with each other. A lot of the
time we shared the same thoughts.
Well, we did back then. These days I
don't know where Dale's coming
from.

It seems weird to say it, but the
best times were when Dad was

injured. Then he'd be around the house for a while. He'd do some of the stuff that other dads did. A minor injury was the best news anyone could bring. Anything more major, though, was really bad news.

It was when he got his broken leg that he started drinking. He got so bored and frustrated. He loved playing football more than anything - more than us, more than Mum. Football was his life.

People say, 'It must have been terrible for you when your dad was doing all that drinking.' But Dad

wasn't violent. He didn't shout or
swear. We just saw less and less
of him. He used to stay out night
after night. When he was at home,
he'd fall asleep a lot. Sometimes
he'd drop off halfway through saying
a sentence. Then the drinking
started to affect his playing. It got
in the papers. Kids at school said
nasty things about him. Dale and
I got into fights about it. I knew
when to stop, when the odds were
against us. Dale never did. And
he's the same now. Trouble follows
him around. Trouble like going
out on the town two days before the

most important match of his life.
Trouble like having too many drinks
and trying to jump a fence for a
stupid dare. Trouble.

Chapter Two

'No,' I said. 'No way. I'm not doing it. This is your mess. You get yourself out of it.'

'Come on Joe,' Dale pleaded. 'My ankle's like a football. No way can I play in two days' time. You know I wouldn't be asking you to take my place if I had a choice.'

'I know you're an idiot,' I said.

'It was an accident, Joe. Anyone can have an accident,' Dale reasoned.

'Yeah but not everyone goes out drinking with their mates a couple of days before the County Cup semifinal,' I said. 'Only idiots do that.'

Dale put on his sulky face. It was a look I'd seen lots of times since we were kids. If you accused him of something, he'd try to make you feel bad. Even if he'd done it.

Dale's coach, Bob Smith, had given him a final warning. If Dale stepped out of line again Smithy would bring in one of the reserves to replace him. If the team won the game, the reserve would play in the final, not Dale.

Dale really wanted to play in that final. There would be premiership scouts there. 'Dale, I hate football,' I said. 'You know that and you know why.'

'Yeah, 'cos of Dad,' he said. 'Don't you think it's time you got over that, Joe?'

Dale had never taken against Dad

for what he'd done. He was always
going round to see him. I haven't
spoken to Dad since he left. My
game was basketball now.

'Besides, this has nothing to do
with Dad,' Dale went on. 'It's me
who's asking, not him.'

He looked at me, pleading. He was the person I cared about most in the whole world, even when he'd done something stupid.

'You want me to do the double,' I said at last.

'Just for a couple of hours,' Dale said. 'You might even enjoy it.'

I doubted that very much. But, as usual, he'd won. When it came down to it, I couldn't say no.

Chapter Three

When I was a kid, my favourite video wasn't Walt Disney or the Simpsons. No, it was Nicky Green's Golden Goals. I used to watch it over and over. I knew each goal

inside out. Dad said I could be a spy
for his opponents.

'I bet you could tell them how to
stop me,' he said.

'No one can stop you,' I told him.
But I was wrong about that. There
was one person who could stop him:
Dad himself. I thought about that as
I tied the laces on my boots. I

wondered what Dad was like at my age. Like Dale probably. He'd have been bouncing about the changing room, joking with everyone, not nervous at all. I was so nervous I felt shaky and sick. I just wanted this to be all over.

'OK, Blackstock, time to get out there and do your stuff,' Smithy said.

The players made their way out onto the pitch. I was at the back. Smithy stopped me.

'You're very quiet today, Dale,' he said. 'Are you all right?'

'Yeah, fine,' I muttered.

'Good. I want to see some real

commitment out there. No switching off when the ball's not at your feet.' I nodded. 'And don't forget - pass the ball. You're not a one-man team.'

'Yeah,' I muttered again. So, Dale was lazy and didn't like to pass. Nothing had changed there then. Well, today, Dale was going to be different.

Chapter Four

Blackstock's opponents were Merton
Athletic. They played in a different
league. They'd won it, just as
Blackstock had won their league.
Both teams wanted to do the double.

I was playing up front, where Dale usually played. Our skipper, Carl, won the toss. He chose to kick off.

'OK, Dale,' Carl said to me as he jogged by. 'Same play as always.'

'Right,' I nodded. But I didn't have a clue what he meant. It made me feel even more nervous. I stood next to the ball, ready to kick off. The ref put the whistle to his lips. Peep!

I froze.

'When you're ready,' said the ref. I tapped the ball forward to my co-striker Danny. In a flash the ball was back at the feet of Carl. He

took one pace forward and booted
the ball upfield. It went straight
to the Merton left-back. Carl glared
at me.

'What you doing, Dale?' he
shouted.

I realised I was supposed to run
forward after kicking the ball. The
Merton left-back was where I should
have been.

'Sorry,' I said, cursing Dale for not
telling me. I felt a right fool.
I made a few more mistakes in the
early stages. I wasn't used to such
a rough game. If you touched
anyone in basketball you gave

away a foul. Football is different. For
the first ten minutes I couldn't get
on the ball.

'Come on, Dale!' Carl hissed
when I'd lost the ball yet again. He
was everywhere - chasing, tackling,
running, passing. I felt tired just
watching him.

At last I got a break. I reached
the ball before my marker. I flicked
it past him, turned and ran. My
football skills were rusty, but I had
pace. I left the defender standing
and ran towards goal.

I might have got a shot in. But
the left-back chopped me down.

Still, it gave us a free
kick in a dangerous
position. And it
got me a
nod of

approval from the skipper.

'Top turn, Dale mate,' he said. He took the kick, but blasted his shot over the bar.

Maybe it wasn't just me who was nervous.

Chapter Five

At half-time the score was nil-nil.

'You all right, Dale?' Danny asked
as we got our drinks. 'You don't
seem yourself.'

'I'm fine,' I said.

Smithy said the same thing. I thought he might take me off. I'd have been quite happy if he had. I'd done my bit for Dale by showing up. Smithy didn't sub me though.

'Bit more effort,' was all he said.

I felt more at ease starting the second half. I'd got used to the pace of the game. My touch was coming back.

In the first minute I set up a chance for Danny. He nearly scored. He should have too. But he hit his shot straight at the keeper.

'Unlucky,' I said.

It got worse. The keeper cleared

upfield. The ball fell at the feet of
a Merton player. He smashed it
past Kola, our goalie, into the net.
1-0 to Merton Athletic. We had
it all to do.

I felt different now. I thought, if

we lose this, then Dale won't be playing in the final. I'd have let him down. This was crazy. After all, I was doing him a favour. All of a sudden, I was full of energy.

'Nice work, Dale,' Carl said when one of my runs won us a corner. Carl took the kick himself. An in-swinger from the left. I jumped. I was ready to nod the ball in the net. Then, *thump!* I was knocked to the floor. That's got to be a penalty, I thought. Then I saw Danny lying next to me.

'Sorry, Dale man,' he said as we got to our feet. 'I thought it was going over your head.'

'It's OK,' I said.

Smithy wasn't so forgiving. Next time the ball went out, he pulled Danny off. He sent on a sub, a skinny kid called Wakim.

'Push right up, Dale,' the coach ordered. 'Let Wakim do the running.' I hoped Smithy knew what he was doing.

Chapter Six

Wakim may have been small and thin, but man could he run! A quick throw down the wing and Wakim was away. He was far too quick for the Merton defenders. They knocked him over and gave away a free-kick.

Time was running out. We were getting desperate. The kick was about twenty-five yards out. Carl placed the ball. I jogged over to him.

'What you doing, Dale?' he asked. 'Get in the box.'

'Let me take it,' I said simply.

'What, you going to take a shot from here?' he said in disbelief.

'Sure,' I said. 'I've scored from there before.'

'When?' Carl muttered.

'Well, a while ago.' I didn't add that "a while" was over two years! I

was good at free kicks then.

The ref blew his whistle.

'Come on, lads,' he called. 'It's your time you're wasting.'

Carl nodded. 'Don't waste it,' he said.

I took the kick. The ball curled round the two-man wall. It zipped towards the near corner of the net. The keeper dived, but the ball was going away from him all the time. It smacked against the inside of the post. Then it pinged over the line.

'Goal!'

We'd equalised and I'd scored. We were back in the match.

Chapter Seven

We were into the last ten minutes. It was still anyone's game. Now I wasn't just playing for Dale, I was playing for me. I wanted to win this match. I'd forgotten how much fun playing football is.

Wakim set up Carl for a chance, but his shot went wide. He was mad with himself.

'Bad luck, skipper,' I said. 'Keep going.'

He gave me a funny look. He wasn't angry, he was puzzled. I guess Dale didn't say things like that.

Now Kola made a fine save. He pushed the shot over the bar. I started to run back for the corner. Smithy shouted at me to stay where I was.

'Keep moving those defenders around,' he called.

I was tired. I wasn't used to running round for this long. The corner was cleared easily. The ball fell to Wakim. I knew what was coming. So did all the Merton players. But there wasn't a lot they could do about it. Wakim was off, flying into the Merton half. Tired as I was, I raced to keep up with the speedy sub.

I knew a cross would come. I had to get into the centre to meet it. I ran so hard, I thought my lungs would burst. When Wakim reached the by-line he pulled the ball back. I dived to meet it. The ball hit me and span past the keeper into the net.

'Goal!'

The ref blew his whistle and pointed to the centre spot. My teammates rushed to congratulate me. This time I held up my hands to push them away. I ran to the ref.

'Well played, son,' he said. 'Nice header.'

I shook my head.

'I didn't head it,' I said. 'The ball came off my hand.'

'Are you sure?' he said.

I nodded.

'From where I was standing it

looked like you'd headed it,' he said.

He blew his whistle again. 'Free kick to Merton,' he said. 'Handball.'

Nobody could believe it. Carl looked at me like I'd turned into an alien. Smithy swore. A lone voice called out from the crowd.

'Well done, Joe!'

I looked round. My heart did a flip. How long had he been there? For the first time in nearly two years, I was looking at Dad.

Chapter Eight

My legs had gone to jelly. My head was on fire. Thankfully, there was no extra time. There'd be a replay the next weekend. If it was still a draw at the end, there'd be extra time and penalties.

As I walked off, the other players ignored me. Smithy was waiting for me.

'What were you doing out there, Dale?' he fumed. 'You let the referee make the decisions.'

'It was a handball,' was all I could say.

'Let him be,' said Dad. 'Cheating's for losers.'

'Yeah, well, you should know,' I muttered. I wasn't thinking about football. I was thinking how he'd cheated on Mum and on me.

'Who's this, Dale?' Smithy

demanded. Then he recognised Dad. 'Nicky Green,' he said. 'You're Nicky Green.'

'Yeah,' Dad said. 'But this isn't Dale. This is Joe.'

Smithy stood there, looking from Dad to me.

'So it was you who called "Joe",' he said. 'I wondered what that was all about. I'm still wondering.'

'Dale's my twin brother,' I said. 'I was doing the double.'

I told them the whole story. Smithy and Dad had a chat when I'd finished. They decided there was only one thing to do. We went off to find the Merton Athletic manager.

'Can we have a word?' Smithy said, smiling uneasily.

'Yeah, sure,' said the Merton manager. But he wasn't looking at Smithy. He was looking at Dad. It's not every day you're face to face with a football legend.

'Good to see you, Nicky,' the manager said.

'Yeah. Good to see you too, Deano,' Dad said. Now it was my turn to look surprised.

'Deano played for QPR,' Dad explained. 'Marked me out of the game once.'

'Once,' Deano repeated. 'Didn't get near you the other times. It's good to see you looking well, Nicky. I know things have been tough.'

It was true. Dad did look well –

much leaner and fitter than when I last saw him. It looked like he'd given up the bottle.

'This is my son, Joe,' he said.

'A chip off the old block, eh?' Deano said. 'Nice goal, son. And an even nicer bit of sportsmanship.'

'Thanks,' I mumbled.

'We've got something to confess,' Smithy said. 'It's about Joe here.' He told Deano everything. Deano looked serious.

'Strictly speaking, I should report this to the League,' he said. 'You could be disqualified.'

'I know,' said Smithy. 'I didn't

know about all this until now. But ignorance is no excuse.'

'You got anything to say, son?' Deano asked me.

'I'm sorry. I really am,' I muttered. I felt awful.

'That was a very good game out there, Joe,' Deano said. 'But for your honesty, your team would have won. Because of your dishonesty, your team could lose. I reckon that balances out. We start again next week on equal terms. I won't take this any further. And I reckon you've learnt your lesson.'

'Yeah,' I said.

Deano smiled. He turned to Smithy. 'I'll tell you something else. You better register this boy quick, before I nab him!'

Smithy laughed and so did Dad. Then he put his arm round my shoulders. My eyes were welling up. I'd missed Dad so much.

'We'd better tell Dale the good news,' he said.

I nodded, too choked up to speak. I had a dad again.

Epilogue

Dale and I both played in the replay. It was like old times. We had an amazing understanding. He knew when and where I was going to make a run. I knew whether he was going to pass or shoot. And Dad was there. During the week, he and Mum had talked in a friendly way for the first time in ages. OK, they weren't going to get back together, but we were all talking to one another. We were a family once more.

Dale and I both scored in the replay. Blackstock Youth won 3-1. Two weeks later, we did it again in the final. We'd already won the league. Now we'd won the cup. That was it. We'd done it. No tricks, no pretending. We'd done the double.

A MURDER OF CROWS

Penny Bates

A Murder of Crows

Some people said there was no such thing as Crow Law.

'It's survival of the fittest,' his daughter said. 'A sick crow is a danger to the flock. So the others finish it off.'

The old man knew better. There were many trials on Crow Hill. Many small skulls lay beneath the trees. It was the way of crows. They always cast out bad blood.

One crow stood on each side of the bird. They pecked out its eyes. Then the rest of the crows dived down. The crow's skull was pecked bare.

'It's not survival of the fittest,' the old man said. 'It's revenge!'

WITNESS

Anne Cassidy

Witness

'Todd Lucas!'

A year twelve was walking towards him.

'I got a message for you from my cousin,' she said. 'His name's Stephen Ripley. He says you know his brother.'

Stephen Ripley? Todd didn't know anyone of that name. Then he remembered. Ripley. Jason Ripley. The man who attacked Mr Wilson.

'What's the message?' Todd said.

'Stephen said you'll be seeing him. Sooner than you think.'

David Orme

Blitz

The shops on the Cut had their windows blown in. People were sweeping up glass and shovelling it into buckets. A copper looked me up and down. There weren't many kids in London in 1940. Most of them were safely out in the country, eating bacon and eggs for breakfast. Sensible kids, not stupid ones like me.

At last I turned into Harrow Street. The school was still there. The houses opposite weren't. No number 18. And no Aunt Josie. And Aunt Josie had never believed in shelters.